BEAUTY
SALON

Mario Bellatin

translated by Shook

Deep Vellum Publishing
Dallas, Texas

Deep Vellum Publishing
3000 Commerce St., Dallas, Texas 75226
deepvellum.org · @deepvellum

Deep Vellum is a 501c3 nonprofit literary arts organization
founded in 2013 with the mission to bring
the world into conversation through literature.

Support for this publication has been provided in part by the Texas Commission
on the Arts.

ISBNs: 978-1-64605-073-4 (paperback) | 978-1-64605-075-8 (ebook)

LIBRARY OF CONGRESS CONTROL NUMBER: 2021940885

Front cover design by Kit Schluter

Interior Layout and Typesetting by KGT

Printed in the United States of America

Any kind of inhumanity,
given practice, becomes human.

—YASUNARI KAWABATA
translated from the Japanese by Edward G. Seidensticker

belly up among the multicolored rocks I'd used to cover the bottom of the tank. I immediately found the rubber glove I used for dye jobs and removed the dead fish. Over the days to follow, nothing noteworthy happened. I simply tried to do things right so that the fish wouldn't die from overeating or hunger. Limiting the amount of food I gave them also helped keep the water consistently clear. But soon the birth unleashed relentless persecution. The other female wanted to eat the newborns. For the moment, their reflexes saved them from death. Strangely, the mother died a few days later. Since giving birth she'd lingered at the bottom of the aquarium, where her swollen belly refused to shrink. I had to put the dye glove back on to remove the dead mother and toss her down the pit in the outhouse behind the shed where I sleep. My workmates never approved of my new hobby. They claimed that keeping fish brought bad luck. I paid them no mind and continued collecting new aquariums along with the equipment necessary to properly maintain them. I acquired tiny pumps disguised as frogmen whose tanks spilled endless bubbles. When I finally achieved a certain proficiency caring for the fancy guppies that I kept buying, I took my chances on more difficult fish. Golden carp attracted my attention. I think it was at the same shop where I learned that in certain cultures the mere contemplation of the carp was a serious pastime. I began to devote hour after hour to swooning over the reflections emitted by their scales and tails. Someone later confirmed for me that such an activity was a strange form of amusement.

But what no longer seems at all amusing is the ever greater number of people who come to the beauty salon to die. It's not just my acquaintances whose bodies are afflicted with the sickness. Now, most are strangers with nowhere else to go. If it weren't for this place, their only alternative would be to perish on the street. Now that the salon has been converted into the Mortuary, the aquariums sit empty. Except for one, in which I try at any cost to maintain some semblance of life. I use the other tanks to store the personal effects dropped off by the relatives of those staying here. To avoid mix-ups I label them with the names of the sick, then fill them with the money, clothes, and confections I occasionally allow. Everything else is prohibited.

But returning to the fish, at some point I also grew tired of keeping solely guppies and golden carp. I think it has to do with a deformity of my personality: I quickly tire of the things I'm attracted to. The worst part is that I then don't know what to do with them. At first it was the guppies, which, at some point, seemed too insignificant for the majestic aquariums that I had in mind to build. Without any remorse whatsoever, I gradually stopped feeding them. I hoped they would begin eating each other. I tossed the survivors down the outhouse pit, as I had the dead mother. That's how I emptied the aquariums to make space for fish that were more difficult to raise. Goldfish occurred to me first. But I remembered that they were very dull, almost stupid. I wanted something both colorful and lively, to pass the time when there were no clients observing how the fish chased each other, or hid among the aquatic plants I'd planted in the rocks on the bottom of the tank.

I did my work at the beauty salon from Monday to Saturday. But some Saturdays in the afternoon, when I was very tired, I left the business to relax at the bathhouse. My preferred local establishment was run by a Japanese family. The owner, a seasoned man of short stature, had two daughters who acted as receptionists. In the foyer they'd tried to respect the Eastern style of the sign on the door. There was a desk decorated with colorful fish and red dragons in bas-relief. The two young women were invariably assembling large puzzles. When someone arrived, they paused their entertainment and took great care to be attentive. The first step was the handover of small, see-through plastic bags, in which the visitor could place whatever valuables they had brought. The young ladies then provided a fob with a number on it, which each person had to hang from his wrist. The Japanese women stored the bag in a given locker and then invited the visitor to pass into the next room. There the decorations changed entirely. The place had the look of the bathrooms at the National Stadium, which I saw once when an amateur footballer had taken me. The walls were half covered with white tiles. Above those, they had painted dolphins, mid-leap. The drawings had faded. I could hardly make out the curve of the animals' backs. In that room the same employee always awaited me to request whatever clothes I was wearing. I always took precaution to wear only masculine garments. After I undressed myself before him, he would stretch out his arms in a mechanical gesture to receive them. He would take note of the number that hung from my wrist and then carry the bundle to the corresponding locker. Before doing so, he would hand me two threadbare but clean towels. I covered my genitals with one and hung the other over my shoulders.

The last time I visited the baths I remembered a story that a transvestite on the street told me one night. He liked to dress exotically. He always wore feathers, gloves—that type of embellishment. He said that some years beforehand, his father had given him a trip to Europe as a gift. He claimed he'd acquired his style during his stay there. In any case, I doubt there's a single person in this city capable of appreciating such fashion. So he would stand on the corner for hours. Not even the patrolmen on their rounds through the district took him out for a routine spin. I was reminded of him because he once told me that his father used to spend the weekends at the steam baths. These were a different kind of baths, quite high-class, not like the Japanese man's. He told me that on one of his first visits, his father's own friends molested him in one of the private showers. He was still a child, and was afraid to tell anyone what had happened. Here—unlike the baths frequented by the transvestite's father—everyone knows why they've come. Once the towels are all that's left covering you, the entire terrain is yours. The only thing you have to do is go down the staircase that leads to the basement. As you descend, a strange sensation begins to pulse through your body. Minutes later you're confused by the steam rising from the main chamber. A few more steps and almost immediately you're stripped of your towels. From there on, anything can happen. In those moments I always felt as if I were inside one of my aquariums. It recalled the murky water, punctuated by the bubbles from the pumps, as well as the jungles created by the aquatic plants. I also experienced the strange sensation experienced when the big fish chase the smaller ones, when they try to eat them. In those moments your limited capacity for self-defense and the inflexible nature of the aquarium's transparent walls become a fully unfurled reality. But those are now times gone by, and I'm certain they will never return. At present my skeletal body stops me from frequenting that place. Another important factor that can now be considered a thing of the past is my enthusiasm, which seems to have left me entirely. It surprises me that I once had the strength necessary to spend entire afternoons at such baths. Even in my best shape, I left a session totally exhausted.

I no longer have the strength to go out looking for men at night either. Not even during the summer, when it isn't so unpleasant to get dressed and undressed behind the bushes in the parks near established meeting places. Because that entire transformation must take place there, and, what's more, in hiding. It would be pure madness to return on a night bus at daybreak, dressed in the same clothes we wore by night. Now I have to run the Mortuary. To provide a bed and a bowl of soup to the victims whose bodies have already been ravaged by the disease. And I alone must do it. The help is sporadic. Every once in a while some institution remembers our existence and aids us with some small amount of money. Others wish to donate medicines. In those instances I have to reiterate that the beauty salon is not a hospital nor a clinic, but rather simply the Mortuary. The rubber gloves are left over from its days as a beauty salon. The jars and clips, as well, and the carts that held the cosmetics. I sold the hair dryers, along with the reclining chairs where we washed hair, to the end of obtaining the tools necessary for the next phase of the salon. With the proceeds from the objects meant for beauty, I bought straw mattresses, iron cots, and a small stove. I dramatically discarded the mirrors, an important part of the salon, which in their moment had multiplied with their reflections both the aquariums and the transformation of my female clients, as they submitted themselves to various treatments. Despite the fact that I'm accustomed to such an environment, I don't think anyone could bear to see the present agony in the salon multiplied in that strange infinity of facing mirrors. I also seem to have become inured to the stench emitted by the sick.

Before becoming a space reserved exclusively for dying in the company of others, the beauty salon closed its doors at eight at night. It was a good time to do so, since many of our ladies preferred not to visit the district where the shop was located any later than that. A sign affixed to the entrance announced that it was an establishment serving both sexes. Nonetheless, never did a single man cross its threshold. Only women seemed unfazed by being served by stylists almost always dressed in women's clothing. The salon was situated at a point so distant from any public transportation line that you had to make a lengthy trek to get there. Two other people worked at the shop, and a couple times a week they accompanied me to the city. We changed, packed our cheap duffel bags, and, after closing our doors to the public, departed. We couldn't travel dressed as women, which was how we performed our services. On more than one occasion, we encountered dangerous situations. That's why we kept the dresses and makeup that we were going to need as soon as we arrived at our destination in our bags. Before going out to wait on one busy avenue or another, dressed again as women, we hid them in the crevices beneath one of the statues of our national heroes. On some occasions all the outfit changes exhausted us, and, if we couldn't actually make any money, we spent time with the patrons of those theaters that continuously project pornography. Our outings through downtown lasted until the early hours of the morning. We returned for our bags and then to the salon to sleep. We'd built a wooden shed behind it, where the three of us stylists slept until midday. We all slept together in one big bed.

At that time my most urgent priority was finding suitable decor for the salon. New shops were opening in the district, which meant that in order to compete a business's look was critical. From the beginning I imagined enormous fish tanks. I wanted our ladies to feel, as they received their treatments, that they were submerged in crystal-clear water, to then break through its surface rejuvenated and beautiful. That's why the first thing I did was purchase a two-meter-long fish tank. I still have it. But that's not where I keep the fish that have survived.

You might find it hard to believe, but I almost no longer distinguish any one guest from the other. I have arrived at a point where they're all the same to me. At the beginning I recognized each one. I even grew fond of some of them. But now they're no more than bodies marching in a deathly trance toward disappearance. I'm reminded of one in particular, whom I knew before he fell ill. He had a gentle beauty, like one of the foreign singers who appear on television. I remember that the queens of the beauty pageants we organized always asked to take her photo beside him. I think he gave the ceremonies a whiff of internationalism. He regularly traveled abroad. It was well known that he had a lover with money who left him when he fell sick. He didn't want to rely on his family. He made up a trip for himself and came instead to stay at the Mortuary. He sold the apartment he owned and turned the money over to me. Before his disease could advance to the point of leaving him in a state of constant delirium, he told me that his frequent trips had not just been for pleasure, but rather that he'd been assigned the task of transporting drugs hidden on his person. He explained to me, in detail, the methods he used to adhere them to his body. I was shaken that someone so beautiful could be used that way. I think it even provoked something special inside me, as I withheld the care that the rest of my guests required to devote myself fully to fulfilling his needs during the time it took him to die. As a special form of deference I placed an aquarium on his bedside table at night. It excited me to note that the boy was not unaware of my preoccupation with him. Somehow he also demonstrated his affection for me. I didn't mind his protuberant ribs, dry skin, or even those vacant eyes, which still held room for pleasure.

It was a little odd that several fish perished at the same time as the boy. While it's true that by then the aquariums' former splendor was long gone, I still kept a fair number of fish alive. Almost all of them were tetras, nicknamed "little nuns" because of their black-and-white coloring, like habits. I don't know—at that time I rejected color. My mood demanded black and white. Each time I think about the boy I took a special interest in, I remember him in his bed with the tank of tetras at his side. Immediately after his death, I found several stiffened tetras on the bottom of the tank. I didn't want to think about anything at all as I removed them. Tetras require a water heater. I'd always had one plugged in. At that time I still adhered to the demands imposed by my aquariums. That's why I consider it more than mere coincidence that they died the exact night the boy passed. The next day I unplugged the heater. Two days later I confirmed that none of them had withstood the water's chill. Some angelfish died, too, after a fungus appeared on their skin. So I went to the store to acquire the same type of fancy guppies that I'd initially had. I put them all into a single tank. They're the ones I'm still keeping. Like I've said, they're hardy fish that have survived more or less the same, despite the minimal care I'm able to offer them: some dying, others occasionally being born. But the water's not as clear anymore. It has taken on a greenish tinge that over time has clouded the walls of the aquarium. I placed the tank in a location at a remove from my guests. I don't want their miasma to sink into the water. I can't stand to see the fish attacked by fungi, viruses, or bacteria. Sometimes, when no one is looking, I lower my head into the tank, even graze the water with the tip of my nose. I inhale deeply, sensing that its water still exudes some life. Despite the odor of the stagnant liquid, I can still discern a certain freshness. What surprises me is how faithful this last brood of fish has proved itself to be. Despite the scant time devoted to their care, they cling strangely to life. They make me think of the curious death of the self typically experienced at the baths. There, too, a prolonged agony of the spirit exceeds the vitality exhibited by its visitors, constantly opening and closing the doors to the individual

But the topic of prolonged agony is of no interest to my guests. For them it is a sort of curse. The shorter the stay at the Mortuary the better. The most fortunate ones spend some fifteen days truly suffering. But there are others who cling to life, just like the last generation of guppies. Even though there's no way to temper their suffering, they persist in their desire to live. Despite the winter cold creeping through the window cracks. Despite the ever-shrinking ration of soup that I serve them. Among my other restrictions, doctors and medicine are prohibited. Also medicinal herbs and healers, and the moral support of friends or relatives. In this regard the Mortuary's rules are strict. Assistance, I've made clear, comes only in the form of cash, confections, and bedding. I don't know where I find the stubbornness to run this place on my own. My companions from before, the ones who worked with me styling hair and doing makeup, died some time ago. Now I occupy the shed alone. I miss them. They're the only friends I've ever had. Both died of the same thing. In their final moments I treated them with the same gruffness as the rest. I still have the clothes we wore on our adventures, hanging on the coatrack. I also keep a box of the trick cards given to us by the men we met those nights. I have never called a single one of them. Not even to inform them why they no longer see us on our usual corners. Although it's likely they don't even remember that we exist. Surely others, younger than us, have now taken our place.

Another reason for my remorse was the expense I incurred on that occasion. Although it wasn't much, it was money that had been given to me for another purpose. I used part of the savings that an old woman had entrusted to me for her youngest grandson. He was a twenty-year-old who had already begun to lose weight. One night I found him trying to escape. He lost his motivation after a beating. He remained prone, peacefully waiting for his body to disappear after passing through the rigorous tortures of the disease. When I returned to the salon with the bag of tetras, very few noticed my acquisition. There were a few guests who had yet to lose consciousness, and I was irritated by their indifference. It seemed to me that they weren't sufficiently grateful, that neither the kind words they or their relatives had used to request their lodging nor their occasional niceties were enough. I needed them to express their gratitude in a more tangible way. For example, by admiring the fish that were still alive, or, perhaps, with some allusion to my body, like making clear that it was still in decent shape.

One time of crisis at the Mortuary was when women came to request lodging. They came to the door in terrible shape. Some cradled their small children, also attacked by the sickness. But I proved myself strict from the very beginning. The salon was once dedicated to making women beautiful; I wasn't willing to let so many years of sacrificial labor go to waste. So I never accepted anyone who wasn't of the male sex. No matter how much they begged and begged me. No matter how much money they offered me, I never said yes. At the beginning, when I was all alone, I started to think about the women who would have to die on the street, many with their children on their backs. But I had borne witness to so many deaths already that I quickly came to understand that I could not bear the burden of responsibility for all of the sick. With time I learned to ignore their pleas, as well as the animus displayed by some others. That, combined with the smear campaign kicked off in the district where the salon is situated, made me fear for my life on more than one occasion.

The campaign unleashed against me was excessive. So much so that, when the public wanted to burn down the salon, the police themselves had to intervene. The neighbors claimed the place was a source of the outbreak, where the plague had come to infest the district. A handful of rocks sounded the first alarm, shattering the glass of the street-facing window. We were scared. There were guests who still had their senses about them and others, worse still, with frayed nerves. It unsettled me to hear their shouting with what remained of their voices. Then began an overwhelming moribund chorus. Outside the neighbors were beginning to force their way in. I had to escape through a hole in the shed where I sleep. I left the guests at the mercy of the crowd. I ran several blocks. It was night. As I progressed, I imagined the neighbors entering the salon, their torches held high. I could see the guests clinging to their mattresses, to their blankets. After an infinite number of blocks, I managed to reach a pay phone. In the notebook that I always carry with me I had several numbers that I'd thought might prove useful. They belonged to the institutions that had always wanted to assist me. After making a couple of calls I continued running until I reached the police station. I had to subject myself to their sarcasm. Until finally a sergeant, who appeared to be more sensitive than the others, heard me out. He listened to part of the story—it's true I did omit certain details—and assigned a group of his men to follow him.

Together we returned. By the time we arrived, the crowd
had managed to break down the main door. However, for
some reason, which I suspect had something to do with
the stench, they hadn't entered. The police fired several shots in the air. The crowd scattered. But my problems didn't end there. The police, who had no previous
idea of our existence, began asking questions. They performed a general inspection. They mentioned the health
code. Happily, at that moment members of the organiza-
tions I'd summoned arrived. They spoke with the offi-
cers. One of them even accompanied the sergeant to
the station. With the others—there were several who
belonged to religious communities—we tried to calm
down the guests. We immediately built a barricade to
get us through the night. Over the days to follow, we did
the work of rebuilding. I fell into a deep depression that,
still, did not make me neglect the guests for any amount
of time. The only difference was that I spent more time

hidden away in my shed. Despite everything, I left early for the market to purchase the vegetables and chicken offal I needed to make the daily soup. Upon returning I took stock of the guests. I cleaned them up the best I could. I accompanied those still capable of standing to the outhouse. Then I got to cooking. In truth, it was not a complicated task. It was just filling the pot with vegetables and offal and leaving them to boil for a couple hours with a fistful of salt. At lunchtime I served their bowls. It was the only food each day. The guests were almost never hungry. Many of them didn't even finish the daily bowl of soup that I placed before them. I ate the same thing. I, too, grew accustomed to doing so only once a day.

Everything appeared to be going well with the pair of aquariums I'd kept alive until, from one day to the next, a fungus appeared on several of the angelfish. At first it was just a few spots growing along their backs. It's strange, the look fish take on in such circumstances. Their colors are obscured by a corona that looks like it's made of cotton. Eventually, most of their bodies were infected and the angelfish would sink to the bottom of the tank a couple days before dying, like the female that had just given birth. To alleviate the feeling provoked by seeing them in such a state, I quickly purchased the guppies that accompany me still. I chose them randomly, without pausing to notice the particular traits of any individual one. As when I acquired my first fish, I chose one male and two females. One of them also turned out to be pregnant. Like I said before, in contrast to my first fish, these did turn out to be hardy. They withstand my unreasonable lack of care. The oxygen pumps are worthless. All but one, which works in fits in starts. The water is only occasionally cleaned. I almost never have time to freshen it. That's why it sometimes gets so low that the fish hardly have room to swim around. When the situation becomes alarming, I fill a receptacle and let the water sit for twenty-four hours. Then I pour it into the tank. Generally, the fish, sluggish from the lack of sufficient liquid, begin to swim back and forth across the tank again. But they do so with great difficulty, as even with the new water the tank is just as green as before. The water is so cloudy that from the outside I can barely make out the shapes in motion, if at all. That's why I've lost count of the precise number of fish still alive.

Some time ago I noticed that the sickness seems to attack in waves. There are seasons when the salon is completely empty. This happens after all of the guests die within a short period and the recently infirm still haven't appeared to replace them. But those periods don't last long. When you least expect it, new guests begin to knock on the doors to the salon again. With a single glance, I can predict how much life they still have left. Their attitude on arrival varies according to their respective dispositions. Almost all of them are dispirited, but some still display signs of light, despite their condition. Others show up completely defeated and can hardly even stand upright. Once they've been interned, I take responsibility for getting them to the same state, no matter their condition on arrival. After a few days, I'm able to establish the right atmosphere. It's a state that I wouldn't know how to properly describe. They become so mired in their lethargy that it's often no longer even possible for them to ask how they're doing. This is the ideal condition for doing my work. It's how I avoid getting involved with any one of them in particular, which makes my labors more expeditious. That's how the work can be accomplished without any type of impediment.

When I had my encounter with the boy who died of tuberculosis, I still hadn't entirely perfected my technique. Although it isn't good to say so, I regret having fallen in love on that occasion. I believe I never should have placed that tank of tetras on his nightstand. Never should have touched him for any motive unrelated to his hygiene. The instance could be considered a mark against my profession. There are some things I haven't recounted, but despite the indifference I displayed when the boy entered the final stage of his disease, I must confess that I secretly worried what kind of burial he would receive. I think perhaps I did so moved by the considerable quantity of money that he'd turned over to me before being admitted as a guest. In this case his body wasn't taken, like the others, to a common grave on the outskirts of the city. I took an interest in his receiving a more dignified burial. I went to a funeral home where I acquired a dark casket. I cleared the furniture from the shed where I sleep and improvised a wake where I was the only mourner. I also hired a black van and secured a burial niche not far from the ground. But I still don't dare go—and I'm almost positive I never will—to the cemetery to decorate his grave with flowers. Like I said, the rest of the dead are taken to a common grave. Their bodies are wrapped in sheets I tailor myself from the fabric that was donated to us. There is no wake. They remain in their beds, until one of the men that I've hired carts them away in a wheelbarrow. I don't accompany them, and when their relatives come to ask after them, I restrict myself to informing them that they no longer belong to this world.

Despite the circumstances, I still feel a melancholy pleasure, to note that, in a certain way, lately my life has some
semblance of order for the first time. Though it seems bit-
ter, the way I've achieved it. My adventures on the streets
have ended, the nights spent in jail after the raids, the
fights with broken bottles sparked when someone tried to
take a boyfriend I'd acquired just moments before. Thos
scenes were almost always incited at the the bars where I
went to enjoy myself. There was one that was my favorite.
The owner had been a friend of mine since I was a boy.
In those days I'd just escaped my mother's house. She
never forgave me for not being the upright son she had
dreamed of. As I had no means of subsistence, someone
recommended I head to the north. At that time, the bar
owner ran a hotel for men, which featured a large dance-
hall on the ground floor. I followed their advice and left.
I couldn't have been more than sixteen years old then,
and I can't complain about my treatment or the amount

of money that I received. The owner, some twenty years older than me, treated me with respect and spoke plainly about a fundamental rule. He told me not to forget for a single moment the fleeting nature of youth. I had to take full advantage of my age at the time. Thanks to him, I managed my finances intelligently. That's how, before turning twenty-two, I could return with the capital I needed to invest in the creation of the beauty salon. I didn't acquire all of the necessary supplies right away. I could only cover the cost of the land and manage to build the main room. At the beginning I only had three or four things, but it quickly became public knowledge that I had a steady hand for cutting hair. That's how my clientele gradually grew and I could purchase the elements needed to make the ladies believe that they were in a high-class establishment. Even so, I felt there was still something missing to make the salon truly unique. That was when I thought of the fish. They would be the touch that gave the shop its special nuance.

But for me personally, things were different. The more stable the business became, the emptier and emptier I felt inside. That was when I began to lead a life you could have called depraved. It's true that I fulfilled my daily obligations, but I was impatient for the days of the week that we'd chosen to hit the street dressed as women. At that time we also began to adopt the custom of dressing that way to attend to the ladies. It seemed to me that we could create a more intimate environment that way. The ladies could feel more at ease. Perhaps then they could share their lives, their secrets. Feel some relief from their problems. But despite the fact that a sort of pleasant unity and harmony developed inside the salon, with the continued abuse of my adventures on the street my life gradually lost something of its psychological center.

When the beauty salon was converted into the Mortuary, I also felt a transformation taking place inside myself. Among other things, as I turned my attention to my guests I became more and more responsible. By then I was no longer so young. For some time my success during our nights downtown had become something of a struggle. I began to experience firsthand the loneliness of my friend who brought his attire from Europe. I had to stand on less exclusive avenues or only conduct my business in the darkness of the theaters. I remembered, those days more than ever, the advice that the provincial hotel owner had given me back then. I noticed his predictions kept coming true, one by one. In contrast, things at the beauty salon kept going better and better. That was the season when the aquariums reached their full splendor. I had a collection of angelfish, goldfish, and pencil fish. I even raised Amazonian piranhas in a tank with several separate compartments. Our clientele grew so much that we had to establish a precise rhythm for our appointments, which was followed religiously. I never allowed a client to arrive late, nor did I pay any heed to those who showed up with last-minute emergencies, nor to those who asked to cut in line.

The man died a month after his intake. I remember our eagerness to restore him to health. We summoned several doctors and nurses. Folk healers, too. We took up collections to purchase his medicines, which were exceedingly expensive. It was all useless. The conclusion was simple. The sickness has no cure. All of our efforts were no more than vain attempts to appease our consciences. I don't know where we have learned that aiding the destitute means attempting to ward off death at any cost. Because of that experience I made the decision that if there was no cure, the best outcome was a quick death, in the best possible conditions for the sufferer. I'm not moved by death in and of itself. The only thing I sought to avoid was for these men to perish in the middle of the street. In the Mortuary they were assured a bed, a bowl of soup, and the company of the rest of my moribund guests. If the guest was conscious, or better yet, still mobile, he could help out, as much morally as physically. Although it must be recognized that the physical help was sporadic at best. It was only given when one or another of them suddenly suffered from an unexpected—and always transitory—recovery, as I always made sure to only accept those with almost no life left before them.

Sometimes vigorous, youthful men knocked at the doors. They assured me they were sick, and some of them even brought the results of the tests confirming it. Seeing them in such condition, it was easy to imagine their undertaking heavy labor. No one would think that death had already chosen them. But though their bodies appeared unaffected, their minds seemed to have already accepted their approaching demise. They wanted to become guests at the Mortuary, at any cost. They even offered to help me with its administration. I had, on such occasions, to muster the same strength I demonstrated to the women who requested lodging to tell them to return several months later. Not to knock on these doors again until their bodies were unrecognizable. With their ailments and disease advanced. With those eyes I now know so well. They were only allowed to return once they could bear it no longer. That's the only way they could aspire to become a guest. Only then could the actual rules I have devised for the correct operation of the salon be put into play. For some unknown reason this type of guest—who'd knocked on the doors when healthy only to be accepted later—was the most grateful for my care. Many of them even praised the aquariums, though there was nothing left within their waters to attract attention.

I felt the first symptoms of the sickness one morning when I woke up later than I customarily do. It was a strange morning. With the first light of dawn I was overtaken by a nightmare. I dreamed that I'd returned to my elementary school, where no one could recognize me. While it is true that I had the same likeness as when I was a child, there was something about me that betrayed how many years had since passed. It was like I was an old man in a child's body. I surveyed my classmates and some teachers. They were the same ones I'd studied with, but they treated me like a stranger, and even seemed to fear me. Eventually, my mother came to pick me up after school, and the same thing happened with her. She came to pick me up and yet couldn't recognize me. I awoke with a profound sadness. Mostly because I'd seen my mother, who died soon after my escape to the north of the country. She was a woman who complained frequently. She always claimed to be sick, and I remember long childhood hours spent in the waiting rooms of large hospitals, accompanying her to one or another of her innumerable exams. When I awoke, I also felt immense anxiety. I stood, left the shed, and splashed water on my face like normal. Then I returned to bed and slept until almost ten in the morning. The sounds coming from the main room woke me back up. The guests were complaining about not being attended to. It was very late by then. Many needed their diapers changed. Others, to be accompanied to the outhouse behind the shed. On one of those trips I noticed the onset of my disease. As I passed the small mirror I kept to shave, I saw two pustules on my right cheek. I didn't need to feel my lymph nodes to know that they were swollen.

Weeks later, my strength began to wane, although not dramatically. At that time I was totally devoted to the Mortuary, but I still reserved an occasional day to go out and have some fun. Sometimes it was a visit to the baths. Others hitting the streets dressed in the clothes that my now deceased coworkers had left me. Still, it wasn't a regular activity. I did it every now and then. But everything came to an end in one fell swoop when I discovered the lesions on my cheeks. The next day I took the dresses, feathers, and sequins to the patio where the outhouse was located. There I made a large bonfire. It smelled horrible. Many of the skirts must have been made of synthetic materials, because quite a toxic smoke billowed up. That day I'd been drinking since early morning. I did so while fulfilling my obligations at the Mortuary. Really, I was capable of completing my tasks in any state. My movements had become sufficiently mechanized that I could perfectly perform my labors guided by sheer force of habit. During the bonfire, I put on one of my friends' dresses. I was totally dizzy, although I'm aware that I danced around the fire while singing a song I can no longer recall. I imagined myself at the bar, dressed in those feminine clothes, my face and neck covered in sores. I intended to fall into the fire. To let the flames envelop me and disappear before the slow agony of the disease could overtake my body. But the song must have blunted my desires. The more I sang, the more clearly I remembered new songs. It kept growing, the sensation that I was entering, bit by bit, the memories they evoked. Slowly, the fire burned out, until it was nothing but a slight wisp of smoke rising from the charred remains. The fire had reached one of the hems of my outfit, and the satin that adorned the dress was completely singed. My hair and eyelashes felt the same. Despite everything I remained on my back, astonished by the fine columns of smoke. The songs had ceased. Other than the sound the fire made, the only perceptible noise was that of the moans emerging from the main room.

Hardly anyone asks about the aquariums anymore, but I would like to say that the strangest specimens I've raised have been the axolotls. They appear to have stopped midway down evolution's path. The specimens I kept were a pinkish white. Their eyes evinced an intense red. They spent the day at the bottom of the aquarium and moved only when I sprinkled the water with the live worms that they preyed on. Many of the ladies were disturbed by their presence. But there were also a few who showed a special interest in them. They must be kept in a special aquarium. They won't tolerate the presence of rocks on the bottom of the tank, nor the plants that I normally use to decorate. I myself must clean the glass with a sponge, as they're so ferocious and so carnivorous that they won't accept—for even an instant—the presence of the janitor fish, among others. Once I conducted an experiment by placing a pair of them in the tank while the axolotls slept. I stayed there for a few moments to witness their reaction. For the first half hour, nothing important happened. The janitor fish began their task and, with their large mouths stuck to the glass, devoted themselves to removing the tank's impurities. The axolotls, as usual, remained at the bottom of the tank. I know that fish, generally speaking, don't know what's happening outside their tanks. Still, as soon as I left the aquarium, the axolotls pounced to devour the janitor fish. When I came back to check on them, the axolotls were back on the bottom of the tank. A few days later they finally tore each other to pieces. After that experience, it never occurred to me to keep them again.

Over the course of these years I've learned that one of the most uncomfortable ways to die is for the disease to manifest in the stomach. It's still a surprise to me why, when the sickness begins this way, the rest of the body seems to be immune to it. When it begins in the head, the lungs, or other organs, it very quickly compromises the other bodily functions. A chain reaction ensues. But with the stomach it seems different. The guest succumbs to a constant discharge that depletes the body, but only to a certain point. The stomach continues to slacken. Meanwhile, their continual deterioration never falters in any significant way. Its rhythm carries on, without apparent highs or lows. Without any sudden distress. The extended discomfort simply goes on. Long, steady. At the Mortuary I've had guests that have endured that process for up to an entire year. And during that period the condition never changes. Still, at no moment do the sick forget that they have no way out. I take it upon myself, moreover, to keep them from harboring false hope. When they believe that they're going to recuperate, I make them understand that the disease treats everyone the same. That those who can't stand their headaches any longer and those defeated by their sores go through a similar process to those who experience long-term, seemingly endless diarrhea. Until a day comes when it appears that the organism has been so emptied from the inside out that there is nothing left to evacuate. Then only the final wait remains. The body falls into a state of lethargy, neither asking nor giving anything of itself. As if in limbo. Generally, that state lasts from one week to ten days. It depends on their bodies and the lives they lived before their time at the Mortuary.

I call it a tedious way to die because it benefits no one for a guest to spend an entire year in such a situation. I have said it many times: there is no greater blessing than a quick death. My guests, like me, are not amenable to that sort of drawn-out death. Occupying a bed for any longer than necessary is taking away that opportunity from another guest who, certainly, will see his brains or lungs attacked before his stomach. From another guest who will fulfill his role and occupy his bed, my time, and my resources no more than necessary. But I've often asked myself what to do when presented with such cases. Finally I reach the conclusion that accepting those who will suffer endlessly with their stomachs is a duty I can't elude. I've placed too many restrictions on myself to impose any more. If the Mortuary won't accept women, children, men in the first stage of the disease, medicines, visits by relatives, the presence of forlorn lovers, medical personnel, reverends, nuns, or healers, I can't also reject applicants whose stomachs are under attack. It seems to me that such an attitude would ultimately pervert the Mortuary's very reason for existing. Following that final rule would make it pointless to maintain the transformation of the salon. It would have been easier to disregard the things happening around me and, unfazed, continue watching both my coworkers and strangers die. The strong young men, the former beauty queens, the boys who sang on television.

The lesions on my cheeks soon covered my entire body. I knew it was unadvisable to rub them with my fingers. Or to treat them with any sort of cream. I'd been told of cortisone's effects on this type of ulcer. Initially it appeared to cure them completely, but after a week they came back with a vengeance. I managed to acquiesce and tried to bear the sores with pride. I noticed several reactions, primarily among the guests' relatives, who only came to the salon to inquire who had died. It was an initial reaction that they then concealed, thinking I hadn't noticed. My body's new state helped me retreat definitively from public life. While it was true that I no longer had the gowns I used to wear at night, I didn't crave a Saturday afternoon visit to the baths, either. Sometimes I imagined the other patrons' reactions at seeing my broken-out body. Most likely no one would notice until they'd been compromised. I'm sure many would flee. Although I'm also sure that others would carry on as if nothing were happening.

The same thing could occur if I dared to go out dressed up at night. Of course in those circumstances it would be different, as it's quite likely that I'd have to confront them face-to-face, with no way out, inside a car or hotel room with some enraged man. At my age and in my condition I was in no shape for those types of experiences. I felt like the fish overtaken by fungus, who scared even their predators away.

On more than one occasion I conducted a particular experiment that clearly proved that sick fish become sacred and untouchable. They're paid absolute respect. A fish with fungus dies only of that illness. Now I'm aware that the same thing will happen to me if I actually hazard a visit to the baths or hit the streets again some night. In reality no one will dare to even approach me, much less expose me to danger. Though it's also true that the behavior of fish doesn't necessarily correspond to that of men. For example, forlorn lovers sometimes try to slip into the Mortuary. They come looking for a guest. I hear them shouting their names in the middle of the night. Sometimes their calls are so loud that many of the sick wake up in fear and commence their usual chorus of moans. I remain in my bed, alert, in case things escalate. The door to the street is reinforced, so it's unlikely that any of the lovers could get in. But still I stay awake. I ask myself at those times what moves those poor creatures to search for the sick. And why come in? Only to find themselves before someone who is no longer a person. Someone who, besides the space they take up, is nothing but a simple carrier of the disease.

It irritated me when those men showed up. Primarily because no one ever came for me. So I ask myself what all this sacrifice is worth. I'm still as lonely as always. Without any type of emotional recompense. Without anyone to come mourn my illness. I believe this is the result of having been so preoccupied with the beauty salon during its days of splendor. And also because of my dedication to my coworkers while they were at my side. If they were still alive, they would worry for me. They would see to keeping me entertained. Perhaps my greatest misfortune is that the disease took my body too late. If I had died sooner, its final throes might have been sweeter. With my coworkers at the foot of my bed, attentive to my needs. But now I must see to them all myself. I must suffer through my decline without uttering a word. There are nights I feel afraid. I fear what will happen when the disease unveils its full splendor. For as much as I've seen countless guests die, now that it's coming for me I'm not sure what's going to happen. Perhaps this is the same feeling my mother experienced when they finally told her, after years of hospital visits, that she had a malignant tumor. I found out while I was working up north. She sent me a letter. I never replied.

Just yesterday, looking at the fish tank with its greenish water, I realized that the disappearance of a fish matters to no one. In all these years the only one affected by the loss of life in the aquariums has been me. I noticed a few guppies hiding among the plants. They emerged, just to return to their hiding. The only reaction that some fish have to death is to eat the lifeless fish. In contrast to the untouchable status of the sick, if the dead fish isn't removed from the tank in a timely fashion, it will become food for the rest. There were times when I purposely left dead ones at the bottom of the aquarium for several days. Each morning I would see how they were disappearing bit by bit. It seemed to me on those occasions that death made a certain sense. But I didn't make a habit of the practice. I almost always removed the fish as soon as I found it. I felt calmer that way, as I sometimes couldn't sleep well at night if I knew a fish was being torn into pieces by one of its previous companions.

Out of respect for the truth, I must admit that the lesions appearing on my body aren't the worst thing happening to me. In extreme cases—an imminent fling, for example—there is always the recourse of makeup. One flesh-tone base coat would be enough to make the irritating patches disappear. Makeup and the assistance of soft lighting. I already tried it once. It's too bad that it wasn't an encounter of that sort, but rather one with the many Sisters of Charity who come to the doors of the Mortuary to offer their services. I don't want them to know I'm sick. I'm sure they would take advantage of any sign of weakness in my command to take the facility over. I won't allow it. I imagine how this place would be if it were run by those sorts of people. Medicines all over the place—uselessly attempting to save lives already chosen by death. Prolonging suffering under the guise of unconditional love. And the worst thing of all, trying to demonstrate by any means how much they sacrifice their own lives by offering them to others. In no way will I accept that in my salon. Some might say that I shouldn't care, but it is something that disproportionately worries me. Even more than the administration of the shop. Perhaps it's because I know that all of the guests will die immediately after I do. And that's not what really alarms me. The sad thing would be how they die. Dying in great bewilderment. The new guests, furthermore, wouldn't be the same. I'm sure that they'll have to undergo testing before being admitted. Some will be remitted to government hospitals. To others, the doors will simply be shut. Most likely they won't want anything to do with the most wretched. Nor with those who behave scandalously, as many of the guests, despite finding themselves gravely ill, never abandon their old habits. Despite their new surroundings, the sort of uniformity I tend to impose, they carry on as always, their manners leaving so much to desire.

I have several ideas, but I don't know if I'll have the strength to execute them when the time comes. The simplest one is to burn down the Mortuary with everyone inside. I know I'll never follow through on such an idea. And it's not just because of potential regret that I reject it, but rather that it seems too simple a way out. Lacking completely in the originality that I've imprinted, from the very first moment, on this place. It also occurred to me to flood it. To turn the salon itself into a huge aquarium. For its absurdity, I quickly rejected that idea. What I do think I'll do is wipe away any trace of it. I must make it as though the Mortuary never existed here. I'll wait until this last cohort of guests dies, and I won't receive anyone else. Little by little I'll reacquire my beauty supplies and return them to their old places. I'll buy hood dryers, a new cart for the cosmetics, and dozens of clips and bobby pins. I'll toss the mattresses and cots into a dump. Also the bedpans and the bowls I use to serve the soup. I'll find an interested buyer for the industrial washer donated to us last month. Not for lack of money, but so as not to raise suspicion by dumping it at some junkyard just because. I reiterate, not for lack of money, since in an economic sense the business has never flourished more than since it became the Mortuary. Between the donations, the inheritances left by the deceased, and the support from their families, I managed to pool together quite a tidy little sum.

What does excite me about the end of the Mortuary is the aquariums recovering their past splendor. I have thought carefully about the steps to take. First I'll rid myself of the tank that contains the last generation of fancy guppies. I'll leave it at the same dump where the bedpans and dishes will go. It'll be so easy to flip the tank over and watch the fish asphyxiate on the rough ground. Once it's empty, I could even start over and fill it back up with the special fish I have in mind to buy. But no, I want to just leave it in the middle of the dump. I'll even replace the water to maximize the oxygen supply for the fish. I'll put in enough food for several days. But then I'll leave the fish in God's hands. Maybe some dog will dip its snout in the waters, or perhaps a beggar will find it. Most likely some peddler of trash will trip over it. I imagine him surprised by the strangeness of his discovery. Then he'll toss out the water and fish so that he can sell the aquarium. By that time, there will already be new fish tanks in the salon, alongside the brand-new beauty tools. There won't be any clients—I'll be the only one. Just me, dying, surrounded by my décor. From time to time I'll muster the strength to reach the sink, where I'll wet my hair. Then I'll place my head beneath one of the dryers. I'll do it all behind closed doors. I won't open up for anyone. Especially not for new guests, whose pleas will penetrate the walls. Nor for the nostalgic lovers who'll knock in exasperation, unable to accept that death has been so ruthless with the object of their desire. Perhaps members of the institutions that make a lifestyle out of helping will come, too. I'll stay quiet and try not to make the slightest noise. I'm sure that after just a few days they'll suspect there's something strange happening inside and will break down the door. They'll find me dead, yes, but surrounded by past splendor.

These are stray ideas that I'll never put into practice. It's too difficult to predict the course my disease might take. I might have some intuitions, but I'm sure that my sickness will chart a different course than the one I've become accustomed to observing for the majority of my guests. It's also complicated to calculate how much time I have left. It's most logical to think that I'll need someone at my side to assist me in my final moments. That's why it's pointless to dismantle this place, which is entirely devoted to the very end of life. Even its decorations. Of them, the fish tank with the green water is best suited to become a dying man's final image. There's nothing that I'll be able to do to free myself from the Sisters of Charity. Most likely, they'll take the reins without my noticing the precise moment it happens. It's even possible that while I'm my final stupor they'll accept new guests without consulting me. I'm sure they'll ignore my rules. They might even be capable of permitting women to come into the salon. I'll hear their endless moans. It'll be a new, exasperating sound. My every intention, twisted. What was once a place devoted strictly to beauty will become a site dedicated to death alone. From then on, no one will appreciate my work, my squandered time. No one will know of my concern that my ladies leave the salon satisfied. No one will understand the degree of tenderness that the boy forced to devote his body to the trafficking of drugs inspired in me; no one the anguish I felt when I heard others's lovers arrive. When I fall sick, all of my efforts will have been in vain. If I reflect more calmly, I think there must have been a moment when I began to feel immortal and didn't know to prepare these grounds for the future. Perhaps that feeling stopped me from taking some time for myself. I can find no other way to explain to myself why I'm so alone at this stage of my life, why no one comes crying for me at night. It's probably just the way I am.

Only recently have I arrived at these conclusions. It's strange to observe how my thoughts now flow more rapidly. I don't think I've ever paused to spend so much time thinking. Instead, I was guided by my impulses. That's how, in my youth, I came up with the money I needed to establish the beauty salon and began going out at night dressed as a woman. But with the transformation of the space, a change took place inside me. For example, today I always reflect on things before proceeding. Then I analyze the possible consequences. Among other considerations, the future of the Mortuary in the wake of my disappearance wouldn't have worried me before. I would've let the guests sort it out as they were able. Now, the only thing I can ask is that they respect the solitude now drawing near.

TRANSLATOR'S NOTE

Reader, I have taken liberties.

PARTNERS

pixel ||| texel

AVAILABLE NOW FROM DEEP VELLUM

FORTHCOMING FROM DEEP VELLUM

SHANE ANDERSON · *After the Oracle* · USA

MIRCEA CĂRTĂRESCU · *Solenoid*
translated by Sean Cotter · ROMANIA

LEYLÂ ERBIL · *A Strange Woman*
translated by Nermin Menemencioğlu & Amy Marie Spangler· TURKEY

SARA GOUDARZI · *The Almond in the Apricot* · USA

GYULA JENEI · *Always Different* · translated by Diana Senechal · HUNGARY

UZMA ASLAM KHAN • *The Miraculous True History of Nomi Ali* • PAKISTAN

SONG LIN · *The Gleaner Song: Selected Poems* · translated by Dong Li · CHINA

TEDI LÓPEZ MILLS · *The Book of Explanations* · translated by Robin Myers · MEXICO

JUNG YOUNG MOON · *Arriving in a Thick Fog*
translated by Mah Eunji and Jeffrey Karvonen · SOUTH KOREA

FISTON MWANZA MUJILA · *The Villain's Dance,* translated by Roland Glasser
DEMOCRATIC REPUBLIC OF CONGO

LUDMILLA PETRUSHEVSKAYA · *Kidnapped: A Crime Story,* translated by Marian Schwartz · *The New
Adventures of Helen: Magical Tales,* translated by Jane Bugaeva · RUSSIA

SERGIO PITOL · *The Love Parade* · translated by G. B. Henson · MEXICO

MANON STEFAN ROS · *The Blue Book of Nebo* · WALES

JIM SCHUTZE · *The Accommodation* · USA

SOPHIA TERAZAWA · *Winter Phoenix: Testimonies in Verse* · POLAND

ROBERT TRAMMELL · *Jack Ruby & the Origins of the Avant-Garde in Dallas & Other Stories* · USA